Can't Catch Me

John and Ann Hassett

Houghton Mifflin Company Boston 2006

Walter Lorraine Books

For Kathy (m.s.)

Walter Lorraine *wn* Books

Copyright © 2006 by John and Ann Hassett

www.houghtonmifflinbooks.com

Library of Congress Cataloging-in-Publication Data
Hassett, John.
   Can't catch me / by John and Ann Hassett.
      p. cm.
   Summary: In this version of "The Gingerbread Man," an ice cube
runs away to sea hoping to grow as big as an iceberg and bump
into boats.
   ISBN-13: 978-0-618-70490-3
   ISBN-10: 0-618-70490-6
   [1. Folklore.]   I. Hassett, Ann. II. Title. III. Title: Can not catch
me. IV. Title: Cannot catch me.
PZ8.1.H2675Can 2006
398.2—dc22
[E]
                                                      2005030852

Printed in China
SCP 10 9 8 7 6 5 4 3 2 1

One hot and sticky day,
a mother made ice for her thirsty boy's lemonade.
She poured cool water into a tray.
She put the tray in the freezer.

"I must go to the store
to buy lemons for your lemonade,"
Mother said to the boy.
"Promise you will not open the freezer door."

But when Mother was out of sight,
the boy forgot his promise,
and he peeked into the freezer.
Out jumped an ice cube.
It ran out the kitchen door.

"Come back," the boy cried.
"You must cool my lemonade."
"Can't catch me,"
the ice cube said. "I'm off
to the sea, where I will grow
as big as an iceberg
and bump into boats when
they are not looking."

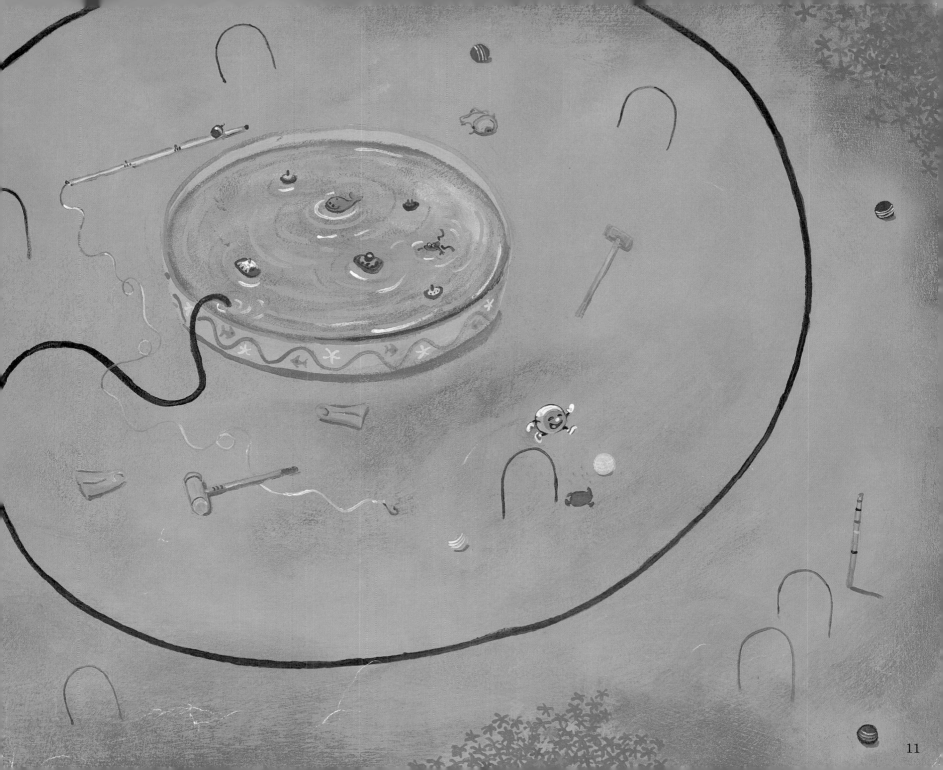

Boy chased the ice cube
past an ant.
"Stop, and I will fetch
my ice skates," said the ant.
"Can't catch me,"
the ice cube said. "I'm off
to the sea, where I will grow
as big as an iceberg
and bump into boats when
they are not looking."

Ant chased the ice cube
past a mouse.
"Soothe my sore tail,"
said the mouse.
"It got caught in a mousetrap."
"Can't catch me,"
the ice cube said. "I'm off
to the sea, where I will grow
as big as an iceberg
and bump into boats when
they are not looking."

Mouse chased the ice cube
past a cat.
"Chill my kittens' saucer
of milk," said the cat,
in hot pursuit.
"Can't catch me,"
the ice cube said. "I'm off
to the sea, where I will grow
as big as an iceberg
and bump into boats when
they are not looking."

Cat chased the ice cube
past a goose.
"Let me swallow you so I will get
goose bumps," said the warmed-over goose.
"Can't catch me,"
the ice cube said. "I'm off
to the sea, where I will grow
as big as an iceberg
and bump into boats when
they are not looking."

Goose chased the ice cube past a popsicle man.
"Hop into my cart," said the man.
"The sun is melting my ninety-nine flavors."
"Can't catch me,"
the ice cube said. "I'm off
to the sea, where I will grow
as big as an iceberg
and bump into boats when
they are not looking."

Man chased the ice cube past a dog.
"Take a rest in my empty water bowl,"
said the hot dog.

"Can't catch me," the ice cube said.
"I'm off to the sea, where I will grow
as big as an iceberg
and bump into boats when
they are not looking."

Dog, Man, Goose, Cat, Mouse, Ant, and Boy chased the ice cube to the sea.
With a wee splash, he dove into the waves.

"Watch for me in the newspapers," he said, swimming the backstroke up the bay.

Out at sea, he felt as big as three icebergs.
He swam past a whale.
"I'm looking for boats to bump,"
the ice cube said.
"Have you seen any?"

Whale was hot and hungry,
and he knew a frosty snack when he saw one.
"My belly is full of boats," he said with a tricky wink.
"Let me at 'em," the ice cube cheered.
"I'll bump them all."

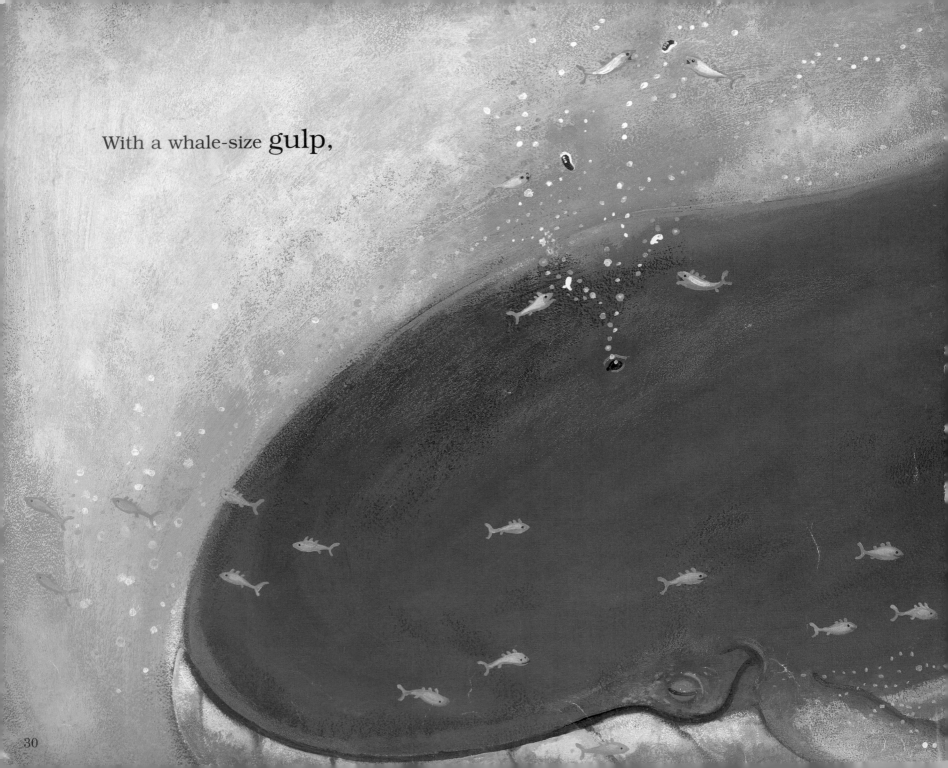

With a whale-size gulp,

the ice cube was gone quicker
than you can say—

"Mother knows best."